D0416512

BIG PICTURE PRESS
www.bigpicturepress.net

First published in the US in 1994 by Prestel Verlag
This edition first published in the UK and Australia in 2013 by Big Picture Press,
an imprint of The Templar Company Limited,
Deepdene Lodge, Deepdene Avenue, Dorking, Surrey, RH5 4AT, UK
www.templarco.co.uk

Copyright © 1994 by The Keith Haring Foundation

1 3 5 7 9 10 8 6 4 2
0513 001

All rights reserved

ISBN 978-1-84877-328-8

Printed in China

This book was typeset in Haring Regular and Keith Regular

Keith Haring

NINA'S BOOK OF LITTLE THINGS!

B P P

The publisher would like to thank Nina Clemente
for allowing her own private book
to be made available to children the world over.

The original book that Keith Haring made
is 12 x 16 inches and was a gift to Nina
on the occasion of her seventh birthday.

A NOTE FROM NINA

I remember drawing a ghost town with Keith on my wall next to my bed. I was scared of ghosts and Keith helped me transition that fear by making all the ghosts look happy and friendly. I also remember giggling with Keith under tables at fancy dinner parties as he told me he wanted to be a pink witch for Halloween.

I don't think I ever realized Keith was an adult. He was a generous companion to so many children, teaching us all a simple lesson of sharing and caring. Not a day goes by that I don't think about how lucky I am to have spent time in Keith's world.

Nina's Book of Little Things was given to me on my seventh birthday and it has since been published in many languages around the world. I am so happy this new edition is available for the next generation of children, as I know Keith wanted everyone to share in his world of drawing, laughter and love.

—Nina Y. Clemente

← NINA CLEMENTE

INSTRUCTIONS

① FOLLOW THESE INSTRUCTIONS

② THIS IS A BOOK FOR LITTLE THINGS. NINA'S LITTLE THINGS. THINGS YOU FIND, THINGS YOU COLLECT, THINGS YOU MAKE, THINGS YOU DRAW, THINGS PEOPLE GIVE YOU, THINGS YOU WANT TO SAVE IN THIS BOOK, BUT — MOST IMPORTANT LITTLE THINGS. IF YOU WANT TO COLLECT BIG THINGS, GET A BOX.

③ PLEASE USE THIS BOOK. DON'T FILL IT UP TOO FAST, BUT PUT IN LITTLE THINGS THAT ARE SPECIAL TO YOU. DON'T BE AFRAID TO DRAW IN THE BOOK. GLUE, PASTE, STAPLE, SEW, HAMMER, ETC. ETC. ETC., TAPE, STICK, ETC. ETC.

④ REMEMBER LITTLE THINGS ARE SOMETIMES THE BEST THINGS OF ALL.

USE THESE 2 PAGES FOR LITTLE DRIED LEAVES IN FALL OR LITTLE FLOWERS IN SUMMER. NO BUGS, PLEASE.

PUT 4 LEAF CLOVER HERE

USE TAPE OR GLUE OR DRAW?

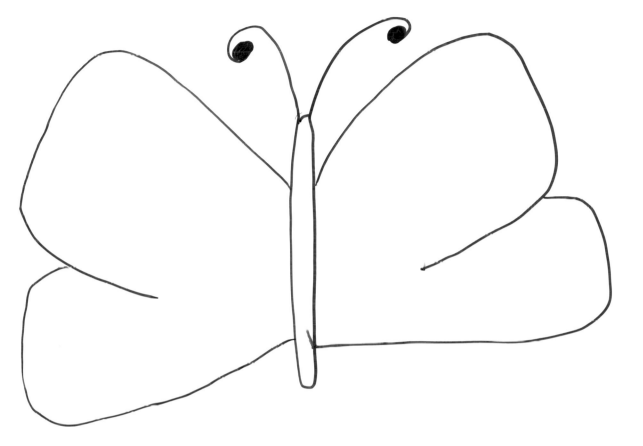

BUTTERFLY
DRAWINGS

USE THESE PAGES FOR SILLY LITTLE THINGS.....

DOG WITH BLACK NOSE

DON'T USE THIS PAGE!!!

JUST KIDDING! HA-HA!

GLUE OR TAPE LITTLE PICTURES

OF LITTLE FRIENDS

OR LITTLE PICTURES OF BIG FRIENDS

OR DRAWINGS OF LITTLE FRIENDS

OR DRAWINGS OF BIG FRIENDS CUT OUT AND MADE LITTLE

OR ....

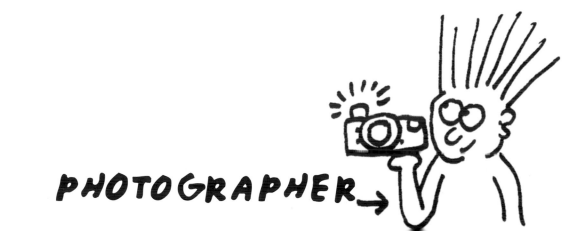

PHOTOGRAPHER →

THE LITTLE MESS PAGE.
I MADE A MESS.
YOU FINNISH IT.
TRY TO TURN MY
MESS INTO A LITTLE STORY.

O.K. I KNOW YOU WANTED SOME PAGES TO PUT LITTLE STICKERS ON, SO, HERE YOU GO!!

LITTLE THINGS THAT FIT INSIDE THIS CIRCLE.

MAKE A LIST OF ALL THE
BIG THINGS THAT YOU WANTED
TO PUT IN THIS BOOK BUT THAT
WERE TOO BIG TO PUT IN NINA'S
BOOK OF LITTLE THINGS.

①

②

③

④

⑤

⑥

⑦

⑧

⑨

⑩

LITTLE THINGS I DID.
LITTLE PLACES I WENT.
LITTLE THINGS I SAW.

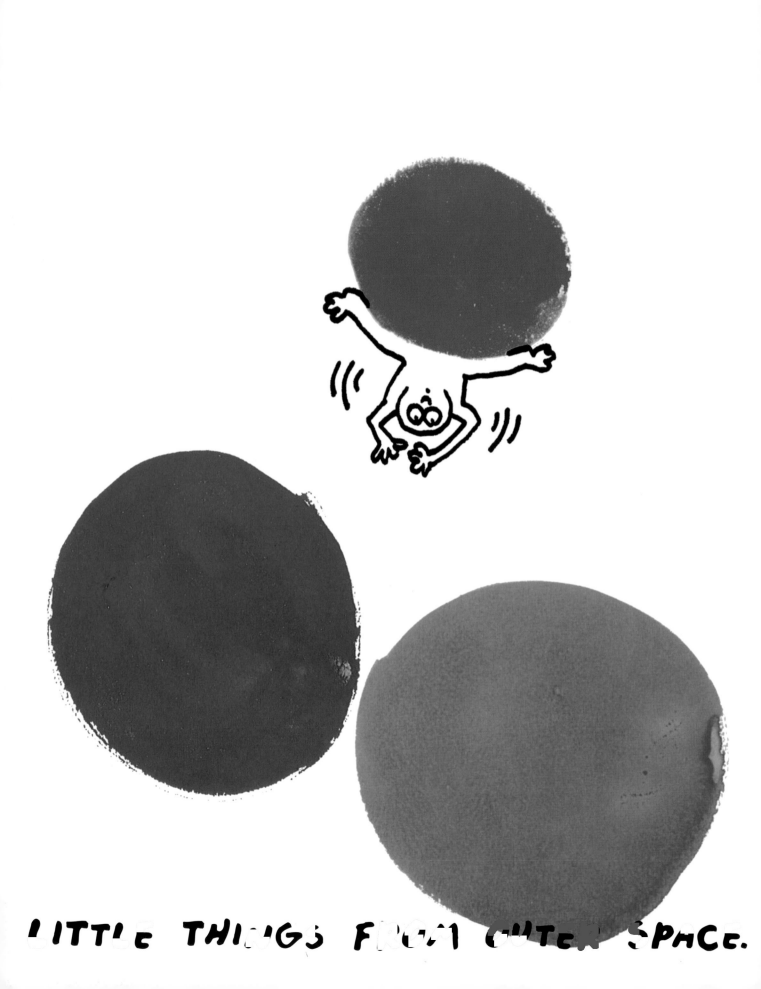

LITTLE THINGS FROM OUTER SPACE.

MY LITTLE SNOWFLAKE COLLECTION

BY NINA CLEMENTE

SNOWFLAKE

← NINA CLEMENTE

PUT
LITTLE PINK THINGS ON
THE GREEN PART.

PUT LITTLE GREEN
THINGS IN THE
PINK CIRCLE.

OOPS! AN EMPTY PAGE.

IMAGINE LITTLE THINGS...

THINGS A LITTLE
BIRD TOLD ME:

THINGS I CUT OUT OF MAGAZINES
AND GLUED ONTO THIS PAGE.
<u>LITTLE</u> THINGS, PLEASE.

← THINKING SCISSORS

THINGS I
FOUND IN ITALY.

THINGS I SAW AT THE CIRCUS.

OR LITTLE THINGS I GOT FOR THIS BOOK WHEN I WAS AT THE CIRCUS.

THINGS I WOULD LIKE TO PUT
INSIDE A BIG BLUE PURSE.

(IF I HAD A BIG BLUE PURSE)

LITTLE
THINGS
I
FOUND
IN
NEW
YORK
CITY.

O.K. , NOW YOU CAN USE THIS
PAGE FOR LITTLE STICKERS IF
YOU WANT TO. BUT, THIS TIME
PUT A LITTLE STICKER DOWN
AND THEN YOU DO A DRAWING
OF THE SAME STICKER NEXT TO IT.

DRAWING OF THAT
STICKER BY
KEITH HARING

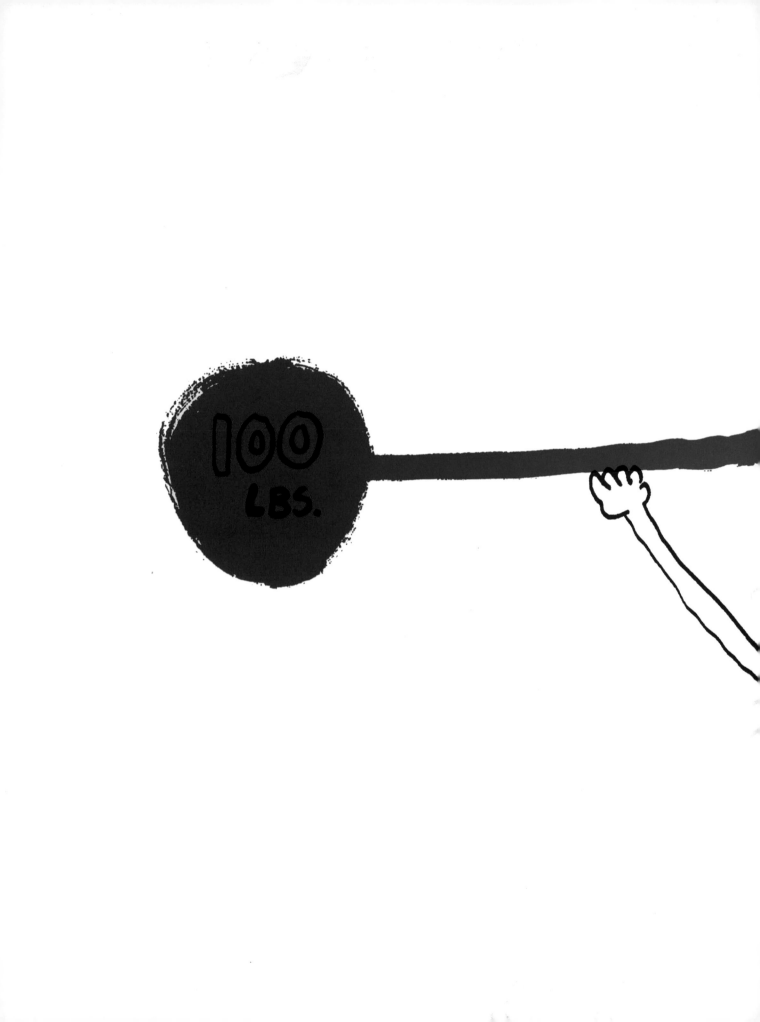

LITTLE THINGS I ACCOMPLISHED.

LITTLE DRAWINGS OF KEITH HARING
CHARACTERS. LIKE THIS →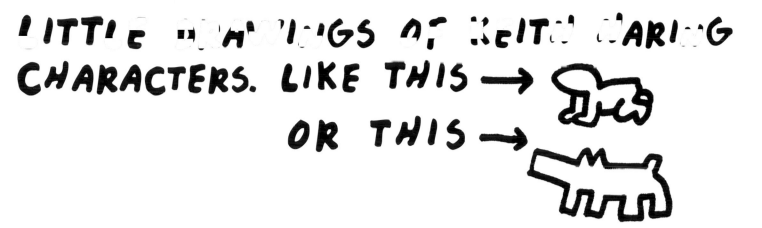
OR THIS →

OR THIS →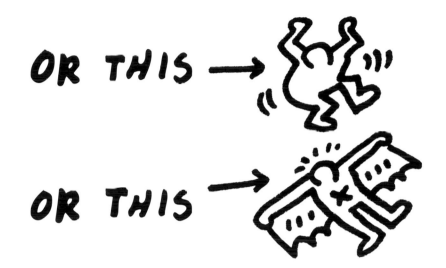

OR THIS →

OR WHATEVER YOU WANT.

LITTLE SONGS I LEARNED.
(THE WORDS OR THE TITLES TO THE SONGS YOU LEARNED)

DRAW THE LITTLE THINGS
THE RABBIT FOUND AT
THE TOP OF THE LADDER.

ANY
LITTLE
THING
YOU
WANT.

ANYTHING!

THINGS THAT BEGIN
WITH "T".

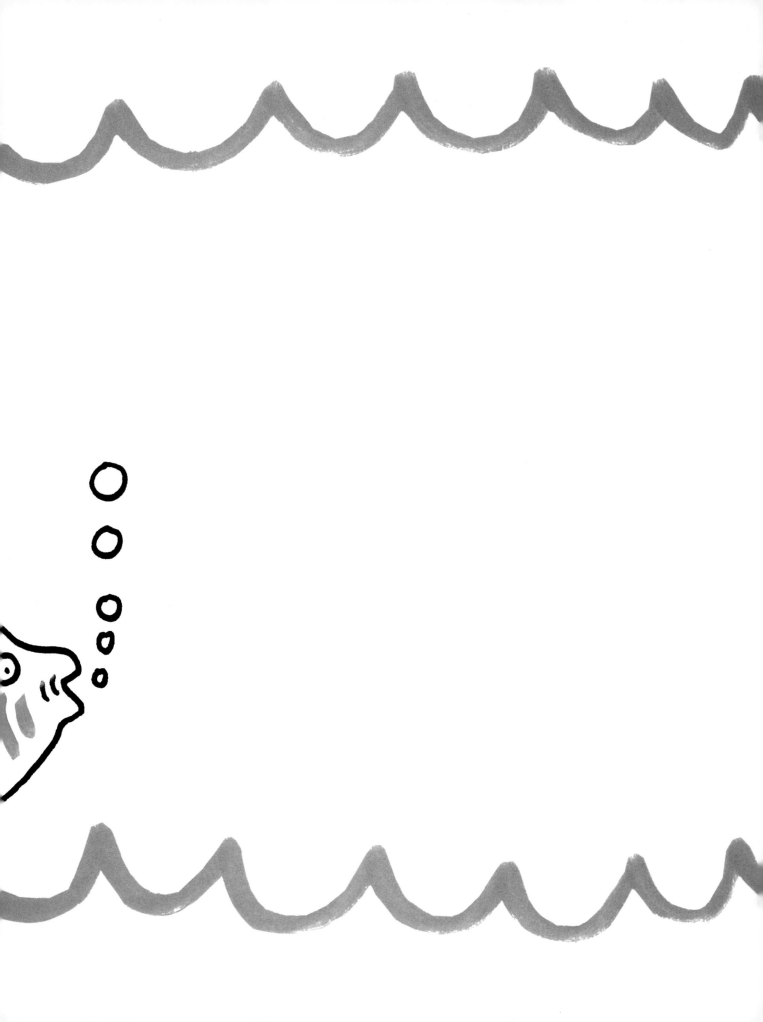

THINGS THAT LIVE IN THE OCEAN.

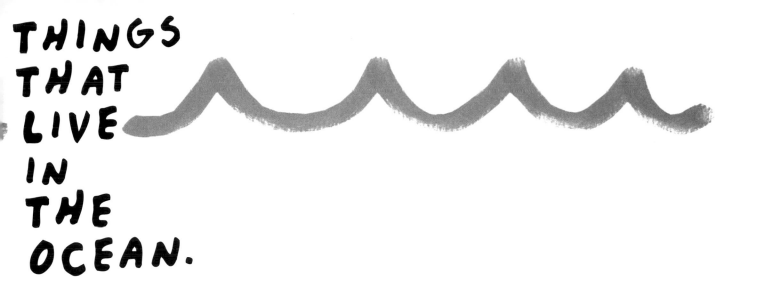

ONLY USE THIS
PAGE WHEN IT
IS RAINING!
DRIZZLING AND SNOW
DON'T COUNT!
RAIN ONLY!

THINGS TO DO WHEN IT RAINS.

PATRIOTIC
LITTLE THINGS.
FLAGS.
STARS.
ANY LITTLE THING
THAT'S RED, WHITE,
AND BLUE.

LITTLE THINGS NINA CLEMENTE THOUGHT ABOUT, WHILE SITTING ON A PINK HILL.

THAT'S IT.

THE END

JULY 14 - 1988 © K. Haring IN NYC ⊕ ◈ FOR NINA—

I HOPE YOU HAD A "LITTLE" FUN — Keith